NOT THAT CLOSE!
JEEPERS! HAVE YOU EVER HEARD OF PERSONAL SPACE?

funny kid

HARPER
An Imprint of HarperCollinsPublishers

funn

**written and illustrated
by Matt Stanton**

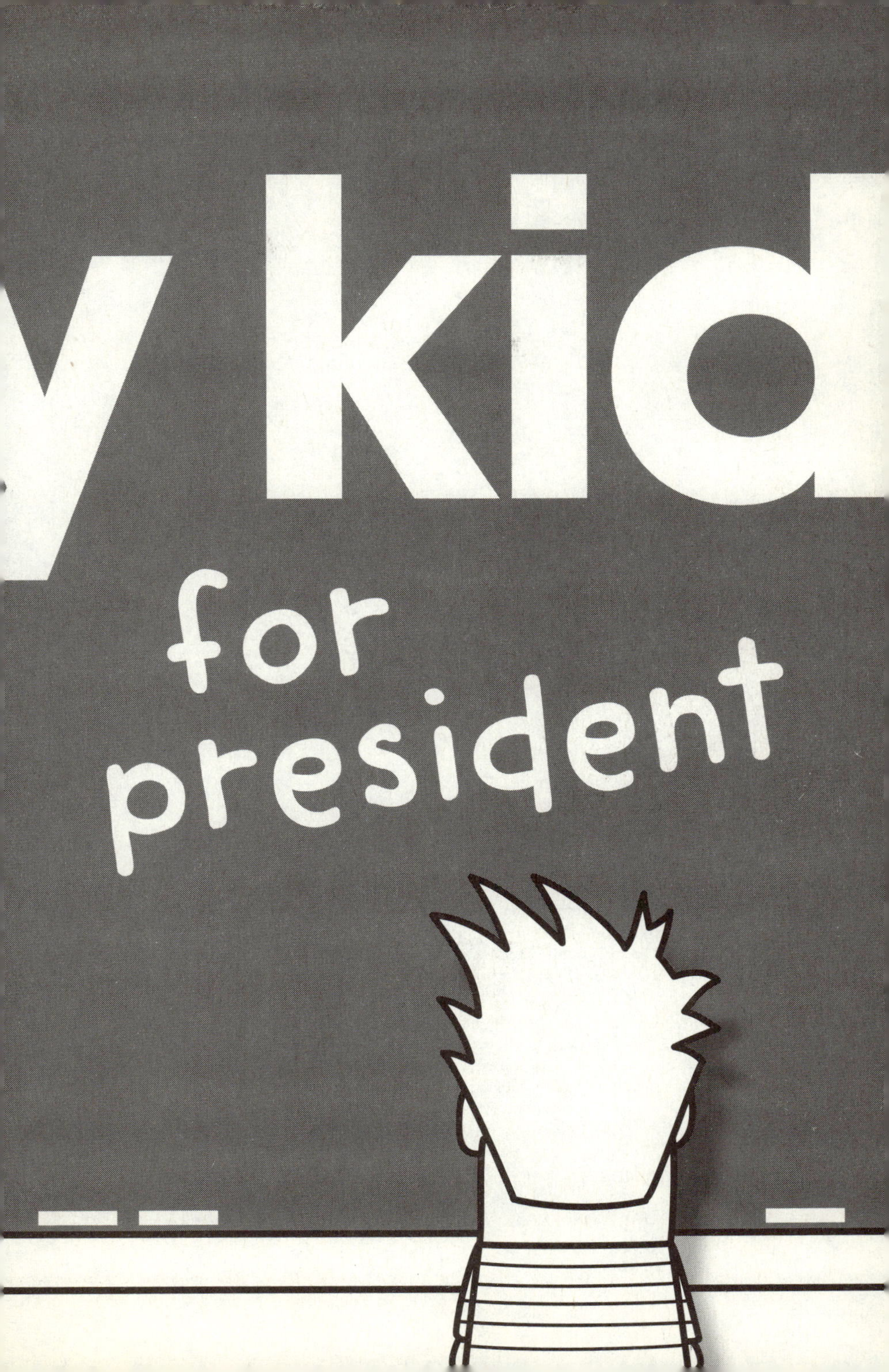

y kid
for president

For Beck, Bonnie, & Boston.

No one can make me smile
the way you three can.

x

1 This first chapter stinks!

Someone has pooped in the storeroom.

Actually pooped. In the middle of the floor. It's lying there in the dark, like a lonely, sleeping baby mole.

That's my teacher, Mr. Armstrong. He's standing in the doorway, glaring down at the little poop like he's going to vaporize it with just the power of his eyes.

Mr. Armstrong doesn't look like a normal teacher. He looks like a hairless gorilla who eats puppies for breakfast. Most teachers look a little, you know … wimpy. Mr. Armstrong looks like he bends iron bars just to relax.

That might sound cool to you. It's not.

Staring at the poop on the floor, Mr. Armstrong is turning the color of a stressed strawberry. Veins pulse in his neck like slugs trying to get away from his face. Normally this means he's about to yell, "TWENTY LAPS!," which means we all have to run around the classroom while he puts "hurdles" in front of us. Take it from someone who's been there, it hurts to crash into a printer and become a human paper jam.

Mr. Armstrong is a volcano that's about to blow. I am seriously considering hiding under my desk. Even on a good day, he explodes at the littlest things – someone forgets their homework (guilty) or forgets their schoolbag (guilty) or forgets their pants (don't judge me!).

WARNING! WARNING! WARNING! WARNING! WARNING! WARNING! WARNING!

But this is a whole new level. I've never seen a head turn red like that. Then again, I've never seen a poop in the storeroom before either.

I'm Max, by the way.

I go to Redhill Middle School, and I'm in Mr. Armstrong's class.

I didn't do the poop.

Mr. Armstrong turns and looks at each of us. For someone with such a big head he has tiny nostrils. They're flaring in and out as he huffs around the room like a gorilla with gas.

"I know you don't believe me, but I can tell who is responsible for that ... atrocity ... just by looking into each of your teeny little eyes," Mr. Armstrong says.

He looks at Emily and Layla, Josh and Ryan. He doesn't seem to think Kevin did it, although I'm not so sure.

Kevin does eat a lot of chili.

Mr. Armstrong stops in front of me.

This is probably a good time to tell you that Mr. Armstrong doesn't like me very much. I think it's because I'm not very good at sports, and to Mr. Armstrong that means there's not much point to me being alive.

"You did the … in there, the thing in the storeroom. You did that."

"No, I didn't," I say. I think it's best to remain calm. After all, I did not do the poop.

"Yes, you did, Max." He puts his hands on his hips and seems to squeeze in his waist. I like to imagine that if he squeezes a bit harder, his head will explode off his shoulders like a popped pimple.

"Really. I didn't do it, Mr. Armstrong." He doesn't seem convinced so I decide to give him a bit more information. "I haven't done a poop since Monday."

And suddenly, the whole class is looking at me in disgust. Too much information?

"That's gross, Max," says the teacher, and he hands me a box of tissues.

"What's this for?" I ask.

"Go get rid of it."

WHAT? I'M NOT TOUCHING THAT! I DIDN'T DO IT! IT WASN'T ME! THIS IS UNFAIR — AND VERY UNHYGIENIC!

(So much for remaining calm.)

"Do it now, Max. Or THIRTY LAPS."

I can't believe it. This is so disgusting. I take the tissue box and drag myself over to the storeroom door.

There's the poop, sitting on the floor all innocent-looking, just waiting for me. I look at the poop. I look at the tissues. I look back at the poop.

"What am I supposed to put it in?"

Mr. Armstrong smirks. "I guess you'd better go get your lunch box."

He thinks he's soooo funny.

2 This chapter is going to get slimy!

I'm walking home from the bus stop with Hugo. I'm Hugo's best friend.

Hugo is a bit chubby and a bit tall and a bit blind and a bit dumb. I like having him around, and I'm even happy to be *his* best friend, but I've told him that *my* best friend position is currently vacant. I'm just waiting for the right person to apply. In the meantime, Hugo is free to fill the role on a temporary basis. He seems happy enough with this.

"Hey, Max," Hugo says.

I'm still fuming about today's poop incident and trying

to think of ways to tie Mr. Armstrong to a rocket launcher and shoot him into outer space. Do I know anyone with a rocket launcher I can borrow?

"Max, we're being followed," Hugo whispers.

Maybe Mr. Armstrong could be the first person to go to Mars … against his will.

I freeze.

I turn around and see that Hugo is right. A few paces back a duck is standing on the footpath, looking at me.

"That's the same duck, isn't it, Max? Your duck?"

I nod. That's the same duck all right.

Sorry, sorry. I just realized you have no idea what I'm talking about. Let me explain.

Most people think all ducks are the same. People think they're harmless little feathered friends. They think they're all adorable and sweet– *WRONG!*

Here are a few things you need to know about *my* little quacker:

DUCK

1. It's not actually _my_ duck. It's just trying to ruin _my_ life. So it's _my_ duck in the same way that you might say it's "_my_ archenemy".

2. Its secret base is somewhere in my backyard. I don't know where exactly because ever since it started trying to ruin my life I've never set foot out my back door again.

3. I think it's armed and dangerous. Well, winged and beaked and dangerous.

4. It has an above-average interest in my ankles (particularly trying to bite them). I mean, I have nice ankles, but this is a little over the top.

PRETTY SURE IT'S PACKING HEAT BACK HERE!

NOT SO INNOCENT!

Copyright: ME

"It must have escaped from my backyard. I've never seen it out in the street before," I say.

"I think it was waiting for you at the corner," Hugo says.

This is not good.

We look at each other. We look at the duck. We look back at each other.

RUUUUNNNNN!!!!!

We make it inside my front door a step ahead of the duck.

The fact that the duck has escaped the backyard and is now stalking me is a rather alarming problem, but it's a problem for another time. Right now we need to work out how to get super-massively-red-face-embarrassing revenge on Mr. Armstrong. Hugo and I start a list:

• Put slime in his protein shake.
• Make him a rat sandwich.
• Put his favorite sneakers in liquid nitrogen so they smash when he tries to put them on.
• Squish one of my sister's dirty diapers into his pencil box.
• Hide three chimpanzees in the back seat of his car.

"We could put a giant spring under his chair," I say. "Then when he sits down at his desk, he'll go shooting straight up and get his head stuck in the ceiling and firefighters will have to come and pull him down, but his head will rip off when

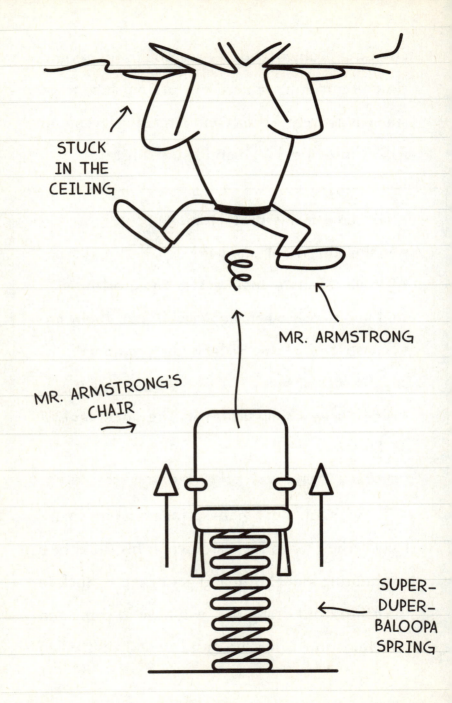

STUCK
IN THE
CEILING

MR. ARMSTRONG

MR. ARMSTRONG'S
CHAIR

SUPER-
DUPER-
BALOOPA
SPRING

they get him free and he'll never be able to teach us again, because he won't have a head."

Hugo looks blankly at me. Brainstorming with Hugo can be a bit one-sided.

In the end, I come up with the best idea ever.

My dad has a worm farm around the side of the house. With real worms in it. Hugo and I spend the rest of the afternoon fishing worms out of the tank and filling a plastic container with them.

Tomorrow, Mr. Armstrong is going to find he has a desk drawer full to the brim with hundreds of juicy, wriggly worms.

At that moment, I know I am a genius.

If Darth Vader and Voldemort had a daughter ...

Before we go any further, there's someone else I need to tell you about. A truly evil villain. More scary than the duck and Mr. Armstrong combined.

Her name is Abby Purcell.

Abby Purcell ruins everything.

Right now Hugo and I are sitting on the bus, going over our plan. I'm whispering because it's a top secret plan. I've seen enough movies that I know that if we were real secret agents, we'd be whispering. Or speaking in code, but I don't know any codes so whispering will have to do.

The last thing we need is Abby Purcell interrupting our secret-agent business.

Which is, of course, exactly what happens.

"What are you whispering about?" she asks.

"Wouldn't you like to know," says Hugo.

"Yes … I would. That's why I asked," Abby says. "Idiots."

"We can't tell you," I say. "It's top secret."

Abby raises only one eyebrow. All evil villains have one magical eyebrow.

LET ME GUESS. YOU'RE HATCHING A REVENGE PLAN TO GET BACK AT THE TEACHER FOR FINDING OUT ABOUT YOUR POOP?

"That. Wasn't. My. Poop."

This is exactly why Mr. Armstrong needs a drawer full of worms. Doesn't he understand how hard it is to be in middle school, let alone if you're known for all eternity as Poop-Boy?

"So, I'm right?" Abby says with a crooked smile.

"It. Wasn't. My. Poop," I repeat.

"Sure, sure. So what are you going to do to Mr. Armstrong?"

"Max has a box full of worms to put in his desk. Look!" Hugo says, pulling open the top of my backpack before I can stop him. There is the box of beautiful slimy worms for Abby to see.

"Hugo!"

"Wow. You've actually put some effort into this," Abby says, looking impressed.

"Isn't it awesome?" Hugo says, beside himself with excitement. "When he puts his hand in his drawer to get a pencil, he's going to stick it right in there. See, feel this –"

He reaches across to my backpack again.

"Hugo – no!" I yell, and slap his hand away like he's trying to steal my cheese balls. "Now

listen, both of you. You can't tell anyone about this, or it won't work. Understand?"

Abby squints. "What are you going to give me?" she asks.

"Huh?"

"What are you going to give me so that I don't tell Mr. Armstrong?" Abby repeats, folding her arms.

Hugo farts a bit. "You wouldn't!"

YOU'RE GOING TO NEED TO BUY MY SILENCE, IDIOTS. YOU HAVE UNTIL THE BELL RINGS TO COME UP WITH SOMETHING. AND IT HAD BETTER BE ABSOLUTELY AMAZING!

Abby Purcell ruins EVERYTHING.

4

Sometimes the toilet is the best place for a cuddle!

It takes us the whole walk from the bus to the classroom to come up with something.

Neither Hugo nor I like having to negotiate with the enemy, but when they blackmail you there's not much choice.

We think of things we can give Abby to buy her silence:

My squished sandwich from yesterday (it's in my bag, under the worms)

Hugo

F–

Hugo's math
homework
(useless anyway)

My little sister,
Rosie

But by the time the bell rings, I have come
up with something better.

"Okay, what are you offering?" Abby asks,
outside the classroom door.

I take a deep breath. "If you don't tell Mr. Armstrong my plan, then Hugo will be your personal slave for a whole week."

Oops. I forgot to tell Hugo the deal.

"Don't worry, Hugo," I whisper. "Trust me."

He looks unsure. Abby smiles.

"That sounds fun," she says. "He will need to carry my bag, wait outside the girls' toilets for me to do my hair, hold my tissues for me when I blow my nose …"

"All that and more," I say.

"Maaaaxxx …" Hugo is tapping my arm. I shrug him off.

"But unfortunately I can't take the deal," Abby says.

"Why not?"

"Max-Max-Max-Max," Hugo keeps nagging. He always does this.

Abby smiles again. "Because I already told Mr. Armstrong your plan."

"*WHAT?*"

"Max! He's coming!"

Storming down the corridor toward us like a bull with a bee sting on its butt is Mr. Armstrong himself. His bald head is tomato red again, his little nostrils are flaring, and his eyes are bulging out and glaring at me!

I turn to Abby in horror. She's doing that lift-one-eyebrow thing like she's going to enjoy watching whatever happens next.

"Why would you do that?" Hugo asks.

She starts to tell us something about truth, justice, and how she wants to see us get squashed like tiny bugs. But I interrupt her speech to yell: "RUN, Hugo!"

* * * *

Hugo and I are cuddling each other on the toilet.

Well, really I'm cuddling him. He's more just crying in fear. Hugo cries all the time. He once cried when he realized that chocolate milk did not actually come from brown cows, and that meant that his quest for the mysterious pink cow of strawberry milk fame was a lost cause.

As for why we're on the toilet, we're hiding from Mr. Armstrong of course.

Slowly we hear the bathroom door creak open. Two heavy footsteps land on the tiles. Hugo looks up at me as if to ask, "When we die, can we keep hanging out in heaven?"

"I know you're in here, Max," the teacher's voice booms.

I look back at Hugo. He's so trusting.

"I have a hostage!" I call out.

Hugo's eyes go wide.

"Don't worry," I whisper. "He's after me."

Hugo starts crying again. I can hear Mr. Armstrong pacing outside the toilet cubicle. Will he break the door down?

"Let him go, Max!"

I'm not sure I've quite thought this through. I try this:

I NEED A HELICOPTER AND TWENTY BUCKS!

"MAX!"

Bang-bang-bang. He's pounding on the door now. I can see the metal hinges straining. Is that a crack in the door?

"MAX!"

Uh-oh.

Bang-bang-bang! That door is going to smash! Suddenly:

WHAT'S GOING ON IN HERE?

Hugo stops crying. Who is that?

"Oh … ah … hello, Mrs. Sniggles," says Mr. Armstrong.

Mrs. Sniggles is the school principal. She's here to save us!

"Why are you scaring the children again, Mr. Armstrong?"

"Mrs. Sniggles, *these* children are going to end up in prison if I don't –"

"Nonsense, Mr. Armstrong," says the principal. "All of you, in my office in two minutes. We're going to discuss this in a civilized fashion. Over a cup of tea."

5 Sniggles, unboxed!

Mrs. Sniggles only started as the principal of Redhill Middle School this year, and this might sound hard to believe, but I've never actually seen her before. Only a few people at Redhill ever have. I only know who she is from the sound of her voice because she addresses the school over the speakers every morning.

There have been many rumors. Some have said that she actually has no body – she's just a granny head connected to a bunch of wires and a big computer. Cyborg-Sniggles never leaves her science-lab office because she can't – she has to be plugged into a power source at all times. She runs the school during the day, and after the bell rings she continues work on building her cyborg army to take over the world.

Theory 1:
CYBORG-
SNIGGLES

Another theory is that she's actually a cat. Cat-Sniggles is a fat feline criminal mastermind who killed the old principal and seized control of the school without anyone ever realizing she's got four legs and a tail. Ricardo in the year above us once saw a whole carton of milk being delivered to her office. He says her signature looks like a paw print. That just about proves this theory, we figure.

Theory 2:
CAT-
SNIGGLES

45

What everyone seems pretty certain about is that as harmless and granny-like as Mrs. Sniggles sounds over the speakers every day, she absolutely has to be a supervillain who is intent on taking over the universe. Either that, or an alien. You decide.

Hugo, Mr. Armstrong, and I approach her office, and the door swings open as if by magic.

"Mr. Armstrong, Max – come in. Hugo, you

can go," says the voice from inside. I turn around and look at my friend. He hugs me and bursts into tears again as though he doesn't want to leave me, but then he runs out of there as fast as his legs will carry him. Traitor.

I follow Mr. Armstrong into the principal's lair.

Only it turns out, it's less of a lair and more of a zoo. The principal's office is jam-packed full of stuffed animals! There are pandas on the bookshelves and lions on the desk. There are birds on the lampshade and bugs in a box. There's a couch with leopard print on it and a pillow with puppies. There's a painting of the Central Park Zoo in New York City on the wall, a rug that looks like a grizzly bear on the floor, and little tiny figurines of whales on the coffee table.

"Have a seat, gentlemen," says Mrs. Sniggles, only I can't see her anywhere. Is she a ghost? That could explain a lot.

Mr. Armstrong and I sit down on the couch, a stuffed giraffe between us, and that's when the tiniest person I have ever seen steps out from behind the desk in the corner and settles herself into a leopard-print armchair. She has gray curly hair, big glasses, and a walking stick. She's wearing a safari suit and hat, and she looks like she's at least a thousand years old.

NOW, MR. ARMSTRONG, WOULD YOU MIND TELLING ME WHAT'S GOING ON HERE?

"Mrs. Sniggles, it's like this. I found out that this little creep here was planning a prank –"

"I don't like that, Mr. Armstrong," she interrupts.

"I know! I didn't like it either –"

"No, no. I don't like you calling a child a creep."

Wait, what?

"But he is one!" Mr. Armstrong exclaims.

"The way I see it, children are our precious little cubs," the principal explains, sipping tea from a flamingo cup. "It's our job to nurture them as they grow. It's a jungle out there."

I smile. I'm beginning to quite like Mrs. Sniggles.

Mr. Armstrong leans forward as though to tell her a secret, but I can still hear him.

"This kid is no *little cub*, Mrs. Sniggles. If he's an animal, he's a pest."

Clink! That's the principal putting her cup down firmly on its pink saucer. She glares at Mr. Armstrong and straightens her glasses.

"I think I'm beginning to understand the problem, Mr. Armstrong."

"Ah —"

"Tell me, who is your class president?" Mrs. Sniggles asks.

"My w-what?" Mr. Armstrong stammers.

"Your class president. Your student representative. I would like to start meeting with you and your class president each week for a little … chat." She is smiling so sweetly, but my teacher is squirming on the sofa next to me. "Is it you, Max?"

"No, Mrs. Sni–"

"We skipped that this year," Mr. Armstrong interrupts. "We just didn't have time in the curriculum –"

He is sweating! I can see drops of Armstrong sweat rolling down his bald head. This is fast becoming the best day of my life.

"Nonsense!" Mrs. Sniggles climbs down from her armchair. "Every class needs a class president. You have one week to hold your elections, Mr. Armstrong. The following Monday I will come and vote myself. After the president is elected, I look forward to a regular cup of tea with you and one of your cubs. I think that should help us all better understand each other. Now hop along, you two bunny rabbits. You have an election campaign to run!"

Mr. Armstrong looks like one pretty cranky bunny to me.

I'm having a lightbulb moment.

A crystal-clear thought.

A gold nugget of genius.

At the same time, I'm running ridiculously fast down my street, trying not to be bitten on the bottom by a surprisingly fast-moving duck, so it's a little hard to concentrate.

Opportunities for greatness don't come along very often, but this is one of those moments. I can get back at Abby Purcell, I can beat Mr. Armstrong, and I can become the most popular kid in my class all in one simple move.

I'm going to become class president.

I can't believe all my problems can be solved so easily.

OOOW

7 A list of people whose butts I need to kick.

Mr. Armstrong lines the five of us up at the front of the classroom. He looks more uncomfortable than ever – like he's hiding a porcupine in his pants.

IT'S A LITTLE SQUISHY IN HERE!

"These shrimps want to be your class president," he announces to all the other kids. He's holding up a bright pink ballot box that he sits on the front of his desk. "They have all of next week to tell you why you should vote for them. The election will be on the following Monday. You should listen carefully to what they have to say ... or don't and just vote for Layla because she's the best."

"What? You can't say that!" That's Abby objecting to things being unfair. I think we can expect this to happen a lot.

"Of course I can. I'm the teacher," Mr. Armstrong says. Abby's mouth is open so wide you could park a school bus in there. Mr. Armstrong sighs. "Okay, I'm just joking. Chill out."

I should tell you about the other candidates—my competition for class president.

LAYLA

Let's start with Layla, the teacher's pet. She's his favorite because she's excellent at sports. It doesn't even matter which sport – tennis, gymnastics, mixed martial arts, or pogo stick races. Her favorite sport is soccer, although she calls it football because her grandparents are Italian. The point is, she wins. She always wins. That's why Mr. Armstrong likes her so much. We once had a running race around the school, and by the time we'd all reached the finish line, Layla had done the race twice, drunk three protein shakes, smashed out 127 push-ups, and beaten all the timekeepers at thumb wars.

Well, Layla, it's time for you to experience the sour aftertaste of being a loser … that someone once told me about.

KEVIN

All the girls love Kevin because he is very handsome – great nose, beautiful bone structure, and the best hair at Redhill. Someone is obviously paying his dentist a lot of money too, because when I'm talking to Kevin, I can just about use those shiny white teeth to check whether anyone is sneaking up behind me.

Kevin, my friend, it's going to take more than style and sophistication and an attractive personality to win this one. It's going to take … smart … things you need to think of … and strategy, you know, ideas and … stuff.

RYAN

Some say that Ryan walks around with his head in the clouds. They're right. This kid can look down his nose at a giraffe. I don't know how you can grow this tall and still be eleven. He's a nice kid and I've always looked up to him (ha!), but this election's going to be about leadership and vision, not just about being head and shoulders above the rest (okay, I'll stop now).

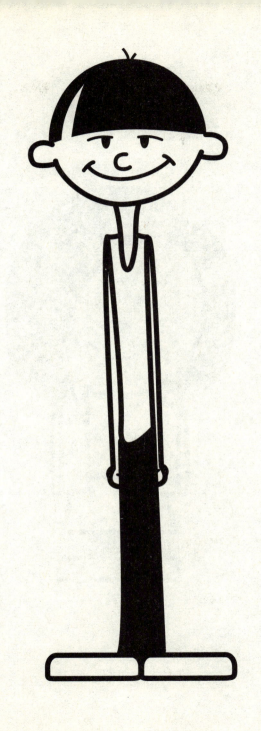

ABBY

Oh. I have nothing to say …

    … about this evil evil evil evil evil evil evil evil evil evil evil evil evil evil evil evil evil evil evil evil evil evil evil evil evil evil very smart evil evil evil evil evil evil evil evil evil evil evil evil evil evil evil evil evil evil evil evil evil evil evil evil evil evil evil evil evil evil evil evil evil evil evil evil evil evil evil evil evil evil evil evil evil evil evil evil evil evil evil evil evil evil evil evil evil evil evil evil evil evil evil evil evil evil evil evil evil evil evil evil evil evil evil evil evil evil evil evil evil bad person.

So here we are, standing at the front of the classroom. The five candidates for class president.

There have been many important rivalries throughout history. David vs. Goliath. Batman vs. Superman. Butter vs. margarine. Right-handers vs. left-handers. Gummy worms

vs. gummy bears. Inevitably things can get ugly when people stand up for what they believe is right. That's what we're doing and I know what I believe is right. It's right that I should be class president.

Hugo gives me a thumbs-up.

He's really going to need to be cooler.

8

Slogans are so cheesy I camembert it.

Hugo and I are getting off the school bus.

"I need you to be my campaign manager," I tell Hugo.

"What is that?"

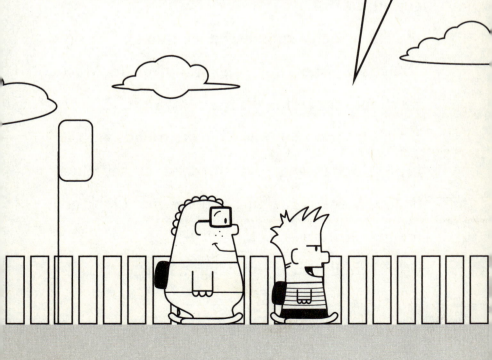

"You sound stressed, Max."

I turn and grab both of Hugo's shoulders and look him in the eyes. "Just focused, Hugo. I'm just very focused. And I'm trying to ignore the duck."

"What? Where?"

"It's right behind you. Don't make any sudden movements."

Hugo turns around slowly and there it is, that stupid duck. It was waiting for me when I got off the bus.

"It is such a cute little duck though," he says. "Maybe we shouldn't run away from it. Maybe we should try and make friends with it."

"I'll show you how to make friends with it." I pick up a twig and throw it at the duck. It dodges the twig and quacks at me. Don't give me that attitude, Duck.

"I think you're annoying it, Max."

I glare at Hugo. "I'm annoying the duck? IT'S annoying me!"

I storm off. Hugo follows.

"Yes, Mr. President."

* * * *

At my place, we have a snack before we start work on my campaign. We need sustenance. I ask Dad to get us some healthy snacks because this is going to be a long slog (over a week) and we need to stay in top physical shape.

We don't have a whiteboard so we draw on the fridge to brainstorm ideas. I'm pretty sure our markers will rub off. Nothing's really permanent, right?

Time to make a list of campaign slogans. People pay a lot of money for good slogans, but we can do it ourselves for free:

MAX RULES!

MAX ROCKS!

MAX ROCKS YOUR SOCKS!

Take Redhill TO THE MAX!

MAX-I-MUM MIDDLE SCHOOL!

"None of these seem right," I say. "We need to inspire people to hope and greatness. It's no good just trying to be funny."

"Wouldn't it be good if it was a little bit funny?"

"No, Hugo. No." I shake my head. "This is very serious. I have to win."

I settle on:

IT'S MORNING
AGAIN IN
MIDDLE
SCHOOL

****

Max for
President

****

"I don't get it," Hugo says.

"Dad said it worked for some old president. Let's go with it," I reply.

Next, it's time to take some photos for the posters.

We hang up a blue sheet in the garage for the background and I dress in my best red-and-white T-shirt. Hugo is going to take the photos on Dad's phone.

"You're not looking very relaxed," Hugo says. "Stretch your face a bit."

"How do you stretch your face?"

"Like this," says Hugo, and he starts grabbing bits of my cheeks and pulling them. Eerrggh. He pushes my nose and pulls my ears.

"Stop!"

We take about 7,000 photos and by then Hugo has to go home. He will probably be busy all weekend designing and printing the posters, and then I've told him to get to school super early on Monday to make sure my posters take all the best spots around the school.

As for me, I'm going to rest. It's hard work running for president!

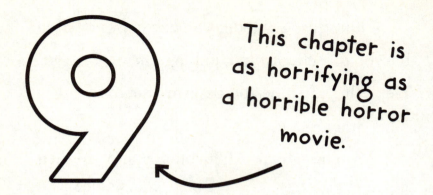

9 This chapter is as horrifying as a horrible horror movie.

I wake up bright and early on Monday. I'm thinking about what Hugo was saying. I think I was a bit stressed last week. It's a lot of pressure running for president – you've got to be "on" all the time.

I decide to start the day by doing some yoga before hitting the campaign trail.

UGH.

Once I'm all relaxed, I untangle myself from my downward-dog pose, get dressed, have breakfast, and head to school. Hugo should have all the campaign posters up by now. When I get there, my face should be covering the halls like wallpaper.

On my way, I run over the day's agenda in my mind.

- An early press conference to talk to the school reporters about my amazing posters and unforgettable slogan.
- Find some babies to kiss (presidents always get their photo taken kissing babies).
- A fund-raising morning tea. (Note to self: only invite the kids with rich parents.)
- More photos with babies.
- Develop a list of reasons why all the other candidates SUCK.

Feeling fired up. Feeling ready to go. This is going to be the best day ever!

* * * *

This is the single WORST day in the entire history of the whole universe.

It's also, I'm quite certain, the most terrible day that will EVER happen at any point EVER – and that includes the day of the *actual* end of the world.

I'm looking at my poster. Hugo has stuck four of them on the school gate. They look like this:

Hugo has used one of the super-ugly stretching-my-face photos on the poster! They're everywhere – on all the classroom walls, doors, and windows, on the flagpole, on the flag, on the teachers' lounge door, on the basketball court, in the garden, covering the disabled parking sign, on all the teachers' cars, on the boys' and girls' toilet doors, on the toilets themselves, in the classrooms, on the desks, on every basketball in the sports cupboard, in the cleaners' cupboard, on the mop, in the hallways, on the ceiling, and on every kid's locker door.

I'm sweating like a pig on a treadmill.

And then I realize Mr. Armstrong is standing right next to me. To my surprise, he doesn't seem mad. In fact, he's smiling.

"Interesting strategy, Max." Then he laughs one of those evil laughs that echoes long after he's stopped actually laughing.

10

Hugo's going to be as dead as a _____!

(INSERT YOUR OWN SIMILE – I'M BUSY!!!)

Sorry, I can't talk right now. I've got to find my best friend so I can PULL HIS ARMS OFF!

When I catch him, I'm going to pop off his legs, plug his ears with his big toes, and push his eyeballs into his belly button. I'll let you know when I've finished.

* * * *

Hugo explains that he accidentally printed the wrong photo on the posters. He fell asleep while everything was printing last night and when he got up he saw his mistake and had to decide whether to put up the posters with the bad photo or not put

up posters at all. He decided it was best to follow my original instructions and put them everywhere.

This was most definitely the wrong decision and he understands this now. So I give him a break and let him keep his arms, legs, and eyeballs in place.

The rest of the day's agenda is scrapped as we deal with the poster crisis. We have to pull all my posters down, only to watch them being replaced with the other candidates' advertisements.

By the end of the day, the other candidates have started writing speeches, making lists of people who promise to vote for them, and handing out flyers. Somehow Abby even has T-shirts made already.

What do I have? A recycling bin full of torn-up posters.

* * * *

At the dinner table I tell Mom about my problems. Mom is a high-powered CEO. She's the boss of a whole lot of people. Kind of like a class president, I guess – just not quite as important.

"That sounds tough, Max," she says, after we've all finished eating. My little sister, Rosie, is trying to stick leftover spaghetti up her nose.

"I don't know how I can win now. All the other candidates have done all this work today

and I've done nothing. Plus, everyone's laughing at me!"

"Maybe that's not a bad thing," says my dad. Dad is an inventor. He makes things in our back shed. That reminds me, I should ask him to invent some duck-proof ankle guards.

"I'm running for class president, not class clown," I reply.

PLUS, THEY ALL THINK I DID THE POOP!

Rosie looks confused. She's usually the one who did the poop.

"What?" Dad asks.

"Never mind."

"It's only the first day of the campaign," Mom says. "We all have bad days. You just have to pick yourself up and take one day at a time. One challenge after the next. What's the challenge right in front of you?"

"Abby," I say.

DEFINITELY ABBY. SHE'LL PROBABLY WIN.

Thanks, Hugo. He's over for dinner. He's been quiet because he's still feeling bad about the poster thing. Nice of him to offer that helpful opinion. NOT!

"So focus on Abby, then," says Mom. "And change the conversation. Get people talking about what you want them talking about."

"Poop," says Rosie, the spaghetti now coming out of her nose and into her ear.

You know what? Rosie might be onto something.

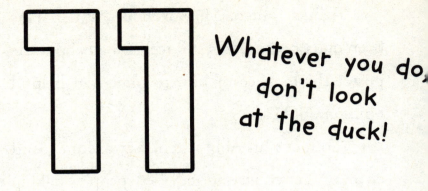

11

Whatever you do, don't look at the duck!

Before school starts the next morning, I have my first press conference. That means I stand on the school steps and start talking to anyone who'll listen.

GOOD MORNING, EVERYONE.
I AM HERE TO ANNOUNCE
THAT I'M RUNNING FOR PRESIDENT.

"Yeah, we know," someone calls out. "We saw your posters yesterday! They were so ugly I've gone blind!"

People laugh. Jeepers, this is tough. I clear my throat.

I'm about to say something presidential when I suddenly see it. The duck. What's my duck doing at school? No one else seems to have noticed it, but I can see it disappearing into the bushes by the classroom. My stalker duck has followed me all the way to school!

Ignore the duck, Max. Ignore it.

"Today is a ... new day ..." Uggghh. That sounds dumb even as I say it. There's a reason they call this a stump speech – I'm stumped!

I notice Abby and the other candidates are standing at the back of the crowd, watching me struggle. Even Mr. Armstrong is there, smiling like a smug hippopotamus.

This is bad. Really bad. What did Mom say? Change the conversation. Make people talk about what you want them to talk about. Okay, here goes.

"Actually, let's talk about the poop," I say. *That* surprises them. Everyone is listening now. "We NEED to talk about the poop. Because we have a pooper among us."

"Yeah, it's you!"

"You think I'm the pooper?" I ask. "So do

most people, including the other candidates. No one can point to any evidence that it was me, just a teacher who thinks that I did it. But it could have been anyone, perhaps even the last person you'd ever expect. It could have been Abby Purcell."

There is silence. I have everyone's attention.

"You know what? I'm glad Mr. Armstrong chose to blame me, because it has motivated me. If you elect me president, I will find the real pooper before they poop again. Even if the pooper turns out to be someone like Abby-pooping-Purcell."

As I look over at the back row, I see Abby glaring at me. I think I can see steam coming out of her eyeballs. I swallow.

"Vote for me as your president, and together we will find tomorrow's pooper, today!"

12

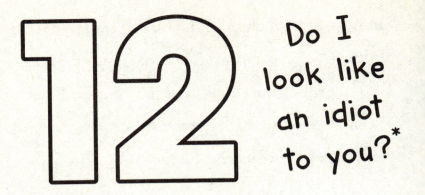

Do I look like an idiot to you?*

It's lunchtime, and Hugo and I are hiding in the library. Now that I know that the duck has followed me all the way to school, nowhere is safe.

We're trying to distract ourselves by coming up with some actual reasons why I should be the president:

*Don't answer that.

On Mondays everyone has to come to school dressed as their favorite cake.

SPORTS WILL BE BANNED.

BURPING COMPETITIONS will be introduced to settle classroom disputes.

I'LL GET ALL THE KIDS SCHOOL SCOOTERS TO RIDE TO CLASS.

I'LL CANCEL THURSDAYS.

I'll give everyone candy canes even when it's not Christmas.

I'll get us a class ~~mascot~~ pet — A KOMODO DRAGON CALLED KENDALL.

I'll make it compulsory for teachers to read us comic books EVERY MORNING.

We are concentrating so hard that when Hugo looks up he screams, scaring the goose bumps off me!

Is someone playing Darth Vader music?

"It's okay, Hugo, it's only Abby," I say. She's standing there, hands on her hips like she's been waiting for us to notice her for the last ten minutes.

"That was quite a stunt you pulled this morning, Max." She always says my name slowly, as though she has a cockroach in her mouth that she doesn't want to squash when she finishes the word. "I'm surprised to see you playing dirty politics this early in the campaign."

"I think you're forgetting this whole thing started because Mr. Armstrong blamed me for the poop. I'm simply sharing the love with my fellow candidate."

"Mr. Armstrong has already said that he thinks you did it, Max. He's going to defend me," Abby replies.

"Good for you. I don't want him on my side. He's the teacher. He's the enemy. If you don't understand that, you'll never be a good president."

"Hmm, brave." Abby shrugs.

I nod. "Mr. Armstrong doesn't scare me."

It's unusual for Abby to pay me a compliment. She must really think …

Hang on a minute, what's going on?

"Wait, why do you think it's brave?" I ask as she starts to walk away.

"Oh, no reason." She stops and looks back at us. "It's just that the teacher has all the power. I think it's smarter to keep the powerful people on your side rather than make them enemies, don't you?"

She's talking in this I'm-so-sweet-I-grow-daisies-and-breed-polka-dot-butterflies kind of way. Time to be the tough guy.

"Well, that's what I'd expect the teacher's puppet to say."

When I say this, I try to do that eyebrow thing she does – raising one up high and keeping the other low – but I just end up doing a very awkward wink.

She does it back, perfectly. *Grrr …*

I'm no puppet, Max. I'm just working hard to be our first girl president.

You'll be the first president, Abby, not the first girl president. There's never been a boy president either, remember.

I go back to writing my list of presidential objectives. I don't have time for this banter with the competition. We're not friends. Abby Purcell is going down.

Hold on, did I just say, "You'll be the first president"?

I look up in horror. Abby Purcell, my evil archrival, is grinning.

THANK YOU, MAX. THAT'S A LOVELY QUOTE FOR ME TO PUT ON MY POSTERS. I'M SO GLAD I CAN COUNT ON YOUR VOTE.

What just happened? How did she do that?

"You make a pretty good puppet yourself, Max." She turns and begins to walk out of the library. "See you at the debate!"

Aarrgghhh ... wait, what debate?

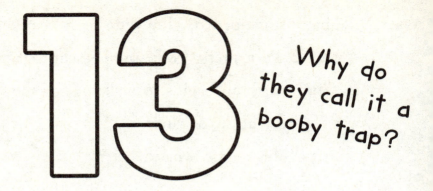

13

Why do they call it a booby trap?

"Welcome to the Class President Debate!"

I've just walked back into the classroom to discover it all set up for a debate. In fact, all the other candidates are already sitting at the front. How did I not know about this?

"Nice of you to join us, Max. Better late than never," Mr. Armstrong says. "Come sit here at the front. The first question is for you."

I look quickly at Hugo, who shrugs as if to say, "This is the first I've heard of it, Max. Believe me, I would have told you if I knew it was happening. This is something it would have been really, really good for you to prepare for."

He has very expressive shrugs.

I walk slowly to the front of the room, feeling more than a little bit anxious. Hugo is right. It would have been helpful to prepare. I'm still feeling rather unnerved by Abby's word games in the library. It's like I've got a tiny little Abby Purcell sitting in my brain, and she's even more annoying in miniature.

I take a spot at the front next to Layla.

"When did you find out about this?" I whisper to her.

"Mr. Armstrong told us all about it after your press conference this morning," she replies.

"He wanted to give us time to prepare. Didn't he tell you?"

I turn and look at Mr. Armstrong. He's glaring at me.

Oh.

Okay.

So this is how we're going to play, huh?

Bring it on.

"The first question is for you, Max," repeats Mr. Armstrong. He is reading from a sheet of paper. "How do you think the science curriculum could be adjusted in the coming weeks so that we can better satisfy the learning outcomes?"

Gulp. He's smiling at me, almost pleasantly. Unless you look at his eyes. They are as cold as a grumpy polar bear eating a flavorless ice block in front of a fan while wearing underpants made of frozen peas and humming "Do You Want to Build a Snowman?"

I have no idea how to answer this question.

"Ah –"

"Can I answer that, Mr. Armstrong?" Of course. It's Abby-the-genius-Purcell.

"Certainly, Abby. Max doesn't seem to be able to."

Abby smiles and takes a deep breath.

There's stunned silence ... then:

"Yes!"

"Woop-woop!"

Of course they would like to make paper airplanes in science lessons. Find me the kid who wouldn't like to do that! It also makes Mr. Armstrong happy because she said the words "teams" and "physics" in one sentence.

The most annoying thing about Abby Purcell is that she actually is a genius.

I'm going to need to lift my game.

"Excuse me, Mr. Armstrong?" It's Abby again. "Can I ask Max a question, please?"

Uh-oh.

"That's not usually within the debate rules," says Mr. Armstrong. "But given Max's unfair attempt to tarnish you in his press conference before school this morning, I'm willing to make an exception."

"Thank you, Mr. Armstrong." Abby looks over at me as if to say, "See?" "Max, I'd like to know what you can offer as president that none of the rest of us can?"

I glance at Hugo. He looks panicked. Thanks for the confidence, buddy.

The truth is, I don't really know how to answer that.

"Um, ah, well ..." What's the best thing to do when you can't answer a question? Turn it

back on the person who asked it! "Before I answer that, Abby, perhaps you can tell everyone what you can offer?"

"Sure, that's easy," she says. "I'm the smartest."

Suddenly I realize what is happening. Abby is trying to end my campaign for president right here in the debate! She's taking the opportunity (after the poster disaster and the poop rumors) to finish me off right here and now. She continues:

"This is not the time for playing games, Max. If we're going to stand before these people and ask for their votes, then we need to be honest. I am the smartest kid in this class and that's why I should be president. Layla is the fastest kid in the class. She is the best at sports. Ryan is the tallest, and Kevin is the prettiest human being that's ever existed. But what are you best at, Max?"

I'm dead. I have no answer to this question because I'm not the best at anything. It's one of those things you secretly realize about yourself and you just hope you can get through middle school before anyone else ever works it out.

Well, Abby Purcell just worked it out! And now she's announcing it to the whole class.

She really is evil.

It can't get any worse than this moment.

Or maybe it can …

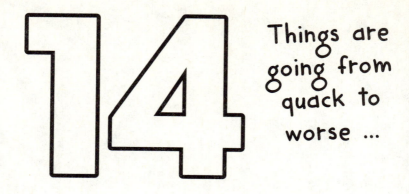

14 Things are going from quack to worse ...

Quack.

Did anyone else hear that? No one seems to be looking around, but I definitely heard it. I scan the room. Perhaps it's just in my head?

QUACK.

Nope. It's here. It's actually here somewhere. Stalker duck. It's heard my voice and found my classroom.

Oh, this cannot be happening right now.

"Max, can you answer the question?" Abby asks.

"Um ... duck," I reply, searching the room for the crazy little bird.

There's an awkward sort of laughter that ripples through the room. I'm looking up to the back of the classroom, past all the kids, trying to see a hint of that beak or get a peek at those feathers.

"What was that, Max?" Abby asks.

Then, I see it. I'm not imagining it. Actually standing at the back of the classroom, finally coming out of hiding, is the duck. And it's looking right at me.

There's more laughter now.

"Mr. Armstrong, I think we need to call the school nurse," Abby is saying. "I think Max is having a mental breakdown. He doesn't seem to be able to handle the pressure."

First, it was Mr. Armstrong out to get me, then it was Abby Purcell, and now a blasted duck has joined the gang! Why? Why me? What did I do to make the world decide to poop on me?

My duck walks slowly toward me, around the legs of kids who aren't paying attention. It's like a cowboy right before a quick draw.

Then, and you're not going to believe this, but like some kind of waddling Abby Purcell, it raises one eyebrow at me! Who even knew ducks had eyebrows?

"Max!" Mr. Armstrong's booming voice breaks through and scares the bottom off me.

Without even thinking, I yell back at him:

THERE'S A DUCK IN THE CLASSROOM AND IT'S GOING TO EAT ME!

Stunned silence. Then …

LAUGHTER!

Duck runs toward me, and I scream a little and dart behind the other candidates.

Quack! Quack! Now everyone's seen the

duck! How could they miss it? It's chasing me around the front of the classroom.

"Help! Help!" I yell as it tries to bite me on the butt. I run down the side of the classroom around to the back of the students. I need a weapon! I grab a chair and turn around to face Duck, holding the chair out in front of me.

Kids are quickly choosing sides. "Max! Max!" "Duck! Duck!"

Quack. It's scratching its little webbed foot on the floor. What? Is this thing getting ready to make a run at me?

YES, IT IS!

Duck charges, and I drop the chair and scream like a baby on helium.

I've done a full lap of the room now, but my duck isn't giving up. It's hot on my tail. Kids are genuinely falling off their chairs laughing.

I'm running backward. I don't want to take my eyes off Duck's beak. That thing's going to hurt if its teeth (do ducks even have teeth?) sink into the creamy flesh of my bottom.

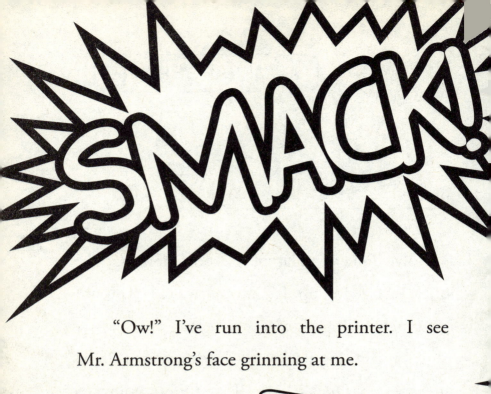

SMACK!

"Ow!" I've run into the printer. I see Mr. Armstrong's face grinning at me.

HURDLE!

Not now, you crazy maniac!

I limp around the printer with Duck hot on my heels. I need a way to solve this problem. I look around for a solution. All I see is a pot of coloring pencils. A bookshelf. The storeroom …

The storeroom!

I run to the door and throw it open, but before I can close it behind me, Duck slips in and bites my bottom.

"Aaarrrggghhh!" My poor left butt cheek!

It hurts so much I let go of the door, effectively locking myself inside, with my duck, in the dark. It's not very big in there. I'm scrambling

around, trying to get the door opened, when –
"Aaarrrggghhh!" My poor right butt cheek!

Duck is behind me now. I manage to grab the handle and open the door just enough to slip back out into the classroom.

The door slams shut behind me and – success – the duck is locked in the storeroom. I slump to the floor, leaning against the door, trying to catch my breath.

But as the sound of blood pumping in my ears quiets, I hear it. Laughing. And not just laughing. Cheering. All the kids are cheering something.

15 I'm having an epifunny!

Someone gives me a high five on the way home.

Kids who aren't even in my class pat me on the back and tell me they heard how funny the duck thing was.

The bus driver says she's heard everyone talking about me today. It makes me smile, because you know what no one is talking about?

Paper-flipping-airplanes.

* * * *

Hugo and I had arranged to meet after school to redo my posters, but as we arrive at my house, I say to him, "Let's scrap it."

"The campaign?" Hugo asks.

"The old slogan."

I grab a piece of paper and a pencil and draw a sketch of a new poster. I slide it across the bench to Hugo. He smiles.

16 Calling all funny kids!

Okay, so here's the big idea for my speech:

I'M NOT THE SMARTEST KID IN THE CLASS. EVERYONE WANTS ME TO BE THE SMARTEST — MY TEACHER, MY MOM, MY FRIEND WHO THINKS THAT GRAMMAR IS THE LADY MARRIED TO HIS GRANDPA. AND I'LL TRY MY BEST. I'LL DO MY HOMEWORK. BUT ONLY ONE KID CAN EVER BE THE SMARTEST. THEN THERE ARE THE REST OF US.

I'M NOT THE FASTEST KID IN THE CLASS. EVERYONE WANTS ME TO BE THE FASTEST — MY COACH, MY DAD, THIS DUCK THAT'S BEEN CHASING ME. AND WHEN THE RACE STARTS, I'LL RUN UNTIL MY LITTLE FEET LIFT OFF THE GROUND — BUT THAT'LL PROBABLY ONLY BE BECAUSE I TRIPPED. ONLY ONE PERSON CAN CROSS THE FINISH LINE FIRST. THEN THERE ARE THE REST OF US.

I'M NOT THE HANDSOMEST KID IN THE CLASS. EVERYONE WANTS ME TO BE THE HANDSOMEST — WELL, OKAY, MAYBE JUST MY REFLECTION. MY REFLECTION WANTS ME TO BE THE HANDSOMEST. AND I'LL BRUSH MY HAIR AND WEAR A CLEAN SHIRT. BUT ONLY ONE KID

CAN EVER BE THE HANDSOMEST.
THEN THERE ARE THE REST OF US.

SO WHAT ABOUT THE REST OF US?
WHAT DO WE WANT TO BE?

I KNOW WHAT I WANT.
I WANT TO BE THE KID WHO MAKES YOU LAUGH.
I WANT TO TELL JOKES.
I WANT TO HAVE FUN.
I WANT TO BURP IN THE QUIZ WHEN WE'RE
SUPPOSED TO BE QUIET.
I WANT TO FINISH THE RACE
WITHOUT CRASHING INTO A PRINTER,
BUT IF I DO, I HOPE IT GETS A LAUGH.
I WANT TO RUN FOR PRESIDENT,
WHILE RUNNING FROM A DUCK.
I WANT TO BRIGHTEN DAYS,
BRING JOY, AND HELP EVERYONE RELAX.
I WANT TO BE THE CLASS CLOWN
OR THE PUNCH LINE.
I WANT TO BE A KID WHO MAKES YOU LAUGH.
I WANT TO BE A FUNNY KID.

FUNNY KID FOR PRESIDENT!

"Bravo!"

"Great speech!"

"Your fly's undone."

That's Mom and Dad. They're sitting on the couch and I've just read them my new stump speech.

Now it's time to zip up my fly, evade a duck, and get out there and win an election.

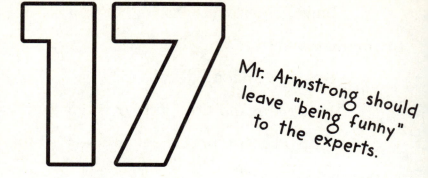

17

I'm standing at the starting line, looking down at the grass and thinking about becoming an ant. Life must be so simple for ants – just keep walking, walking, walking and follow the bottom in front of you. What an easy life!

Unless your buddy in front is farty, I guess. Still, I'd consider trading lives with an ant right about now if it meant I could get out of Mr. Armstrong's Presidential Race.

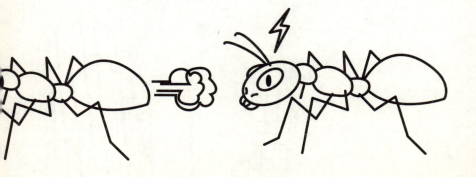

I don't mean the election, I mean an actual running race.

I hate running. I hate it like fish hate skateboarding – it's not natural! When God was making my body, he'd run out of ingredients by the time he got to my legs. They're the legs of a much shorter, lazier person. They're way too short to get the rest of me moving at any reasonable pace.

"Get set!"

Besides, what is the point of running anyway? Haven't we invented enough things that enable us to move faster if we need to – scooters, cars, rocket launchers? Choosing to run is like choosing to ride a horse to the store – we've found a better way, people!

But Mr. Armstrong is convinced that it would be fun to have an actual Presidential Race. That's his idea of funny. He's lined up all the candidates at one end of the sports field and he wants us to run to the other end while everyone watches.

He's about to yell, "Go!" when I realize my shoelace is undone.

"Time out!" I shout, reaching down to fix it.

"Too late, Max!" replies Mr. Armstrong. "GO!"

Wait! What? No!

The other four candidates take off, but I'm half bent toward my shoe. Without asking for permission, my legs decide they're going to run too.

It happens in slow motion.

1. My right knee comes up and hits me in the nose.

2. My head flicks back, which means when my left leg launches forward it flips straight up in the air.

3. Instead of running, I am now doing a backward somersault.

I'm looking at sky. I'm looking at clouds. I'm looking at Mr. Armstrong upside down. I'm looking at grass. I'm looking at an ant's butt. So, this is what it feels like.

I flop onto the grass and look up just in time to see the rest of the candidates reach the finish line. No surprise, Layla's clearly in front.

Me, on the other hand? I think I actually moved backward.

Clap. Clap. Clap.

"Nice one, Max," says Mr. Armstrong as he steps over me. "You're doing a really good job of losing this all by yourself, aren't you?"

He chuckles a little, and then yells to the rest of the kids. "Back to class! I bought lunch for everyone!"

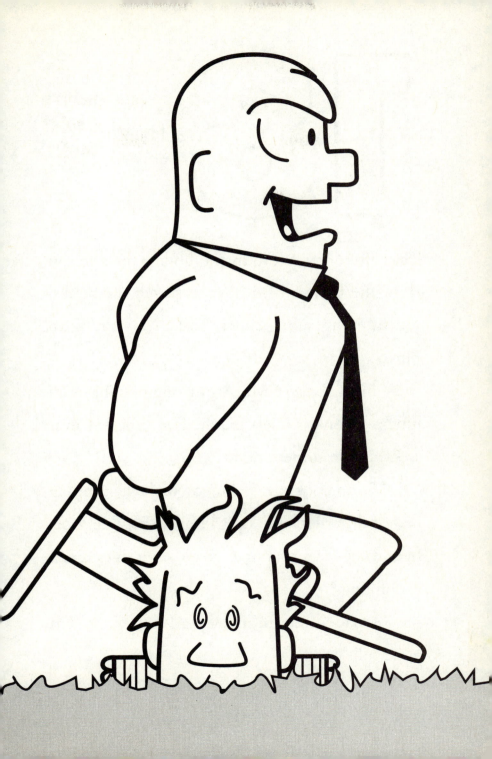

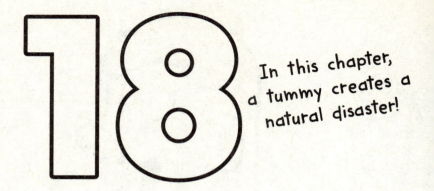

18

In this chapter, a tummy creates a natural disaster!

That afternoon, we're in the library for a lesson from the librarian on how to search for books. I'm listening super, super hard. And talking to Hugo.

"I can't believe Mr. Armstrong bought us all lunch. I think it might be the first time I've ever seen him do something nice," I say.

"I don't know," Hugo replies, rubbing his tummy. "I'm still a bit hungry. Fat-free, nut-free, dairy-free, taste-free green smoothies aren't very filling."

"I had a mouthful of grass earlier, so I'm quite full."

Everyone laughs. It was Kevin – the style king himself.

"He looks a little gray," says Hugo. He's right. Cute Kevin's not looking so hot right now.

"Kevin, are you all right?" Abby asks.

Then it happens. It starts as a low rumble from somewhere, like a distant plane or a groaning rhinoceros that doesn't want to do its homework. Then Kevin begins to wiggle – up and down, left and right – and he starts to get that panicked look in his eyes. The one that says, "Something very bad is about to come out of my body, and I'm not going to be able to stop it."

During a natural disaster, people need their commander in chief. Someone who's not going to panic. It's time to step up.

"He's going to blow!" I shout. "Everyone down!"

People begin to scream, but it's too late.

Green-smoothie spew projects out of Kevin's cake hole like water from a hose, spraying on the bookshelves as he turns like one of those creepy clowns at the community fair.

We hit the floor, but what goes up must come down – vomit included.

"Get behind the shelves!"

I grab Hugo and drag him behind a shelf.

"I'm hit! I'm hit!" the librarian shouts.

We look out from our shelter behind the dictionaries. Sure enough, the librarian has taken it in the face. She's going down.

I peek through a gap in the books just as Kevin turns in our direction!

I dive backward, grabbing Hugo and Abby on the way down.

SPLASH!

Vomit hits the shelves, and a few splatters sail over our heads. If anyone wants to find "spew" in the dictionary now, they'll have no trouble.

We stay pressed against the stacks, close to the floor, catching our breath. Everything is eerily silent.

When it feels safe, I sneak a peek. The library has been painted green. There are bodies everywhere. I spot Kevin lying still, moaning softly, looking emptied – like a shriveled balloon.

I hold a hand out to help up Hugo and Abby. "You're my hero," Hugo says.

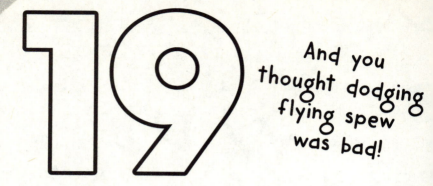

19

And you thought dodging flying spew was bad!

Vomit-apocalypse was bad. Kevin was sent home sick – out for a week, according to his doctor. It turns out he's lactose intolerant, and even though Mr. Armstrong's smoothies were *supposed* to be dairy-free, they didn't go down well. (Or come up well, for that matter.) That means Kevin will probably miss the election, but either way, it's a bit hard to ask someone for their vote after you've spewed in their face.

Call me brutal, but this is a good thing as far as I'm concerned. There's one less person to beat now. Politics is a contact sport.

When I get to school the next morning,

everyone is buzzing. Apparently Layla is going to make a shocking announcement before class.

"Maybe she's going to tell us that she's an alien," I suggest to Hugo.

"Yeah!" he says. "Or a turtle."

Sometimes I really wonder if Hugo's brain is actually a giant clump of chewed gum.

We gather at the bottom of the steps, and sure enough, Layla stands up in front of everyone to make her announcement.

"I have something shocking to say," she says. "Really shocking."

Yep, we've got that.

IT'S ABOUT MAX.

Wait, what? I thought this was going to be about her.

Hugo nudges me and winks. "That's you," he whispers.

He looks excited. Idiot. This is going to be bad.

"Max said that he did not do the poop."

Uh-oh.

"He said that there was no evidence that he did the poop. But he has been lying to you."

Suddenly everyone is turning and looking at me.

"Ah, no, I haven't," I manage to mumble.

"Lyin' Max, that's what we should call him," Layla says, and all the kids laugh.

"He didn't lie!" Hugo shouts.

WHAT'S YOUR SHOCKING EVIDENCE?

A hush falls over the crowd as everyone turns back to Layla.

"There is a video."

Everyone gasps.

MR. ARMSTRONG HAS A HIDDEN SECURITY CAMERA IN THE STOREROOM JUST IN CASE SOMEONE TRIES TO STEAL SOMETHING. HE CHECKED THE VIDEO ON THE CAMERA, AND GUESS WHAT? IT SHOWS MAX DOING THE POOP. NOW, IS THIS REALLY WHO YOU WANT AS YOUR PRESIDENT? THE STOREROOM POOPER?

I'M DEAD.

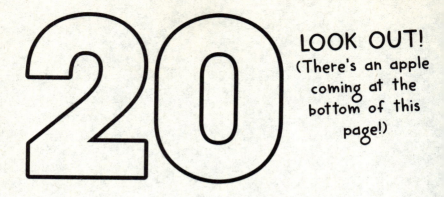

20

LOOK OUT! (There's an apple coming at the bottom of this page!)

The dictionary says that a scandal is any event that causes public outrage.

As Hugo and I run away from the crowd of kids chanting, "Lyin' Max, do we trust him? No, we don't! Is Max the storeroom pooper? Yes, he is!", it occurs to me that this probably counts as public outrage. The only way to make this worse would be if people started throwing stuff.

OW!

Okay, an apple core just hit me in the head.

I think we have a political scandal on our hands.

We're going to need a plan.

* * * *

Hugo balances his dad's phone on the table and turns on the video camera.

"Are you sure this is a good idea, Max?"

I check my hair and sit up straight in the chair. "There's only one way to respond to a political scandal," I explain. "You have to do a tell-all interview."

"And you want to put it on YouTube?"

"Layla claims Mr. Armstrong has a video that no one's seen. We'll give everyone a video they can actually watch. Are we rolling?"

Hugo nods.

"Time to ask me the tough questions, buddy."

He coughs a little bit.

Hugo looks confused. "But you're not talking to the voters. You're talking to me."

I make sure I keep smiling. The camera is filming my every move.

"Well, yes, but I'm talking to them through this interview."

"That's a bit silly. Why don't you just actually go and talk to them?"

My mouth is still smiling, but I am glaring pure hate at Hugo now. I suspect I look like a zombie who's had plastic surgery.

"You're a voter, Hugo. I'm talking to you, aren't I?"

"So, are you going to do an interview with everyone, then?"

"HUGO!" I explode. I turn off the camera. "What are you doing?"

"You said, 'Ask me the tough questions.' Were they too tough?"

"About the poop, Hugo. Ask. About. The. Poop."

"Oh …" It's like turning the lights on for the poor guy. "Sorry, Max."

We start again, and Hugo gets straight to the point this time.

"Tell us once and for all, Max. Did you do the poop?" Much better.

"Hugo, I want to say one thing to the students of Redhill Middle School and I want them to listen to me because I'm not going to say this again." I am using my don't-mess-with-me voice. I want to sound as much like a president as possible. "I did not do the poop in that storeroom."

HOW DO YOU EXPLAIN THE VIDEO, THEN?

I CANNOT EXPLAIN IT, HUGO. I DID NOT DO THE POOP SO I CANNOT BE IN THAT VIDEO. HAS ANYBODY ACTUALLY SEEN THIS VIDEO?

I BELIEVE MR. ARMSTRONG HAS SEEN IT.

IS IT?

WELL, THAT'S INTERESTING, ISN'T IT.

"Why would Mr. Armstrong tell everyone that there was a video of me doing the poop when there isn't one?"

"I ... ah ... do you want me to answer that?"

"Why don't I answer it?" I say.

I lean forward and look directly into the camera. Here it comes:

WHOEVER SMELT IT, DEALT IT.

21

If you thought he hated me before ...

It's interesting to see what happens when you suggest to a group of kids that their teacher may have pooped in the storeroom.

We upload our video the next morning, and the gossip circles around the school in about three and a half minutes.

> APPARENTLY IT WAS MR. ARMSTRONG ALL ALONG!

> HE'S BLAMING IT ON MAX TO COVER IT UP!

> IF WE VOTE FOR MAX AS PRESIDENT, HE WILL PROVE THAT MR. ARMSTRONG IS THE REAL POOPER!

"Mr. Armstrong is going to eat you for lunch," Hugo says.

* * * *

Mr. Armstrong doesn't wait until lunch to eat me. He takes our class to the gym early, but as I head out the door, he grabs my collar and holds me back.

> MAX, MAX, MAX.
> CAN I TELL YOU WHAT I FEEL
> LIKE DOING AFTER WATCHING
> YOUR LITTLE INTERVIEW?

I'm not sure I'm supposed to answer that. He's waiting a really long time though. Maybe I am supposed to answer it. I'll answer.

> SURE.

> SHUT UP, MAX!

155

I wait for him to say something about pulling out my intestines and feeding them to the duck. Actually, it'll probably be worse than that. He'll want to put my intestines on coat hangers on the back of his car, hanging down like sausages. Then he'll put ketchup on them, because my duck probably likes ketchup, and he'll drive his car down the street with my intestines flapping in the wind and the duck chasing us. He'll say "us" because he'll think I'll be in the back of the car, watching my duck chasing my intestines down the street, shouting:

STOP, DUCK! DON'T EAT MY INTESTINES!

Mr. Armstrong will be laughing and laughing, which he'll blame me for because, apparently, I'm the funny kid.

I'm about to point out that there's a problem with his story, because if he pulls out my intestines I'll be dead, so I won't be able to watch the duck eating my intestines, when I realize that he didn't actually say any of that.

Instead he's saying something about how I need to quit running for president.

"Why?" I ask.

"Because you're going to lose. There's no point trying something if you can't win," he says.

Teacher of the Year Award over here, please. Anyone? Anyone?

"How do you know I can't win?"

He gets really close to me then. I can see the tiny hairs on the top of his nose and smell the garlic smoothie he had for breakfast.

"Because I'm the teacher, Max, and as the teacher I'm going to use every bit of my biceps, every string in my hamstrings, and every try in my triceps to make sure you don't win. Do you really want to go to war with me, Max?"

You might think I'd be terrified in this moment, and you'd be right. But what you can't see is that there's a little bit of snot at the end of Mr. Armstrong's nose, and it's hanging on to a nostril hair that he forgot to trim. I'm only half listening to his threats because I'm watching this tiny piece of snot hang on for dear life (and frankly, because I'm scared that it's going to come flying through the air and hit me in the face).

BBBBRRRRRIIINNNNNGGG!

Saved by the bell!

22

Anyone
need a
pep talk?

The bell ringing means that it's time for Mr. Armstrong to actually start our basketball class. He lines us all up on the court.

"As I've told you many times before, gym class is not about everyone having a turn," Mr. Armstrong begins. "It's not about doing your best. It's certainly not about feeling part of a team."

He paces up and down in front of us. I look at Hugo. Why do I feel like gym class is going to be worse than normal?

"Life is about winning," Mr. Armstrong continues. "Sports are about winning. That means that sports are life."

I remember Abby trying to argue this logic with him once. She didn't get very far.

"It's my job to teach you to be winners. Look at Layla, for example." No one looks at Layla. "Layla is a winner. She's fast. She's driven. She's coordinated. I'm sure she'll be your next class president, and she deserves to be. If only you could all be winners like Layla."

Abby raises her hand, as she always does when she thinks he's said something unfair. Mr. Armstrong ignores her, the way he always does when he's said something unfair.

"The best way to teach you to be winners is to remind you over and over again how humiliating it is to be a loser."

He certainly knows how to give a great motivational speech.

Mr. Armstrong then goes on to explain today's drill. We will be learning how to do alley-oops, which, true to form, are almost impossible for an eleven-year-old to do.

Mr. Armstrong has a catapult machine that shoots basketballs up in the air in front of the hoop. We will have to run, jump on a small trampoline, fly through the air in front of the hoop, catch the ball in midair, and dunk it in the basket. All we have to do then is land without breaking an ankle.

Layla goes first, of course. She runs like a cheetah, bounces like a kangaroo, flies through the air like an eagle, and dunks the ball like an NBA star. Thanks, Layla.

Hugo is next. He runs like a hippo, bounces like a bowling ball, loses his glasses as he flops forward, and lands on the ground like a dead person. The basketball bounces off his bottom and rolls to the other end of the court.

Abby is supposed to be next, but she has a note from her mother excusing her from such exercises, much to Mr. Armstrong's disgust.

Ryan is next, then it will be my turn. This is bad for me because Ryan is actually built like a basketball player. He could probably dunk the ball without using the trampoline.

I, on the other hand, will have trouble jumping high enough to get on the trampoline.

"Ryan, go!" shouts Mr. Armstrong.

I watch, feeling like I know exactly what's going to happen. Only, I'm wrong.

Ryan runs, jumps onto the trampoline, and flies higher than anyone else has so far. The next part happens in slo-mo. The ball shoots out of the catapult, and rather than being at the right height for him to catch, it smacks him straight in the head.

Ryan drops like a rock.

23

See? Sports ARE bad for your health.

At the risk of sounding like Mr. Armstrong, there are winners and losers when it comes to today's basketball mishap.

Ryan is obviously a loser because he had his head smashed by a giant orange ball. He broke his nose, was mildly concussed, and will be off school for at least a week.

LOSER

Which is one of the reasons why I am a winner. If you can't remember which day of the week it is, you can't really convince someone to vote for you. I'm crossing Ryan's name off my list of reasonable competitors. I'm also a winner because Mr. Armstrong had to stop the basketball drill after the accident and I never had to humiliate myself on that stupid trampoline.

* * * *

"Hey, what happened to your posters?" Hugo asks at lunchtime.

"What do you mean? We put up the new ones two days ago."

"Yeah, but they're not there."

I look to see where Hugo is pointing. The wall beside the hall is covered in Abby's election posters. But there's a gap between each poster where another one used to be. Mine!

"Someone's been pulling down my posters!"

We walk around the corner and sure enough, my posters are gone from the bathroom doors and from the locker room too. I also notice a couple of Layla's have been ripped down and left on the hallway floor to rot.

"I know who did this," I say.

"You do?"

I turn to Hugo. "Look whose posters haven't been touched."

* * * *

People are looking across the playground as we shout at each other underneath a tree.

"Why do you think it was me, Max?" Abby asks.

"You didn't think it through. Your posters are the ones that are left."

"Some of Layla's are still up."

"If it was Layla, she would have pulled down both our posters." Sometimes I wonder if Abby thinks I'm stupid.

"You're stupid, Max," Abby says. "Don't you guys understand what is going on here?"

"What are you talking about?" Hugo asks.

"Mr. Armstrong. His fingerprints are all over this."

I shake my head. "Don't try to blame him."

THINK ABOUT IT, MAX! IT WAS MR. ARMSTRONG'S IDEA TO HAVE A PRESIDENTIAL RUNNING RACE THAT LAYLA WAS ALWAYS GOING TO WIN. AND WHO WOULD HAVE KNOWN THAT KEVIN WAS LACTOSE INTOLERANT? MR. ARMSTRONG, BUT HE STILL GAVE KEVIN THE SMOOTHIE THAT MADE HIM SPEW. YOU ALMOST GET KNOCKED OUT OF THE COMPETITION BECAUSE MR. ARMSTRONG TELLS LAYLA HE HAS A SECURITY VIDEO PROVING YOU POOPED IN THE STOREROOM, AND THEN HE ORGANIZES A BASKETBALL EXERCISE THAT ACTUALLY KNOCKS OUT RYAN. WHICH LEAVES YOU, ME, AND THE TEACHER'S FAVORITE LEFT STANDING.

"And now he wants you and me to turn on each other," I realize.

"So that Layla will sail home to victory," Hugo finishes.

Unbelievable. Mr. Armstrong is rigging the election! If he is going to be forced to sit down

every week with Mrs. Sniggles and the class president, then he wants to make sure he gets to decide who that class president is.

"The problem is, we have no actual evidence," Abby says.

"Then we're going to have to find some."

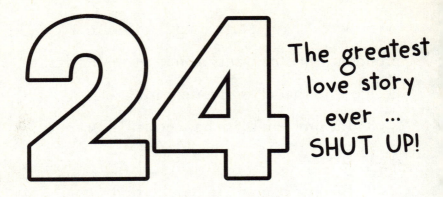

24 The greatest love story ever ... SHUT UP!

There's a branch poking me in the armpit.

Every time I try to push it back, another one slaps me on the head as if to say, "Push one of us and you'll deal with all of us, buddy."

I'm in a shrub, by the way. We all are – Hugo, Abby, and me. We've been sitting in a shrub for ten minutes. My shins are getting itchy, and a ladybug just climbed into my T-shirt.

"Stop grabbing my leg, Max!" whispers Abby.

"That's not your leg! It's a branch from the – oh, sorry, it is your leg."

It's after the bell's rung and everyone's left for the day. Everyone except Mr. Armstrong. We're

waiting for him to go so that we can sneak into the classroom and search for evidence. My old posters in his desk drawer would be perfect.

I'm still fighting with the armpit branch when I hear something.

Quack.

Oh, you've got to be kidding me.

"It's your duck, Max!" whispers Hugo.

"Seriously?" I turn around and realize there aren't three of us in this shrub, as I originally thought. The number is actually four.

"What is your problem?" I hiss through gritted teeth. "Not now, you evil feathered fiend!"

Abby sighs. "You're such an idiot, Max."

"Just give me a break, would you?" I knew we shouldn't have brought her along.

"You want to know what the duck's problem is, Max?"

"What would you know about it?"

"It thinks you're its mother."

What? *WHAT*?

Hugo starts laughing in that muffled way that sounds like you're farting out of your mouth.

"Tell me, Max, where did you first see the duck?" says Abby in that know-it-all tone of voice she has.

"Ah, um, in my backyard. It came out of a bush one day. When it was really little."

"Like a little duckling?"

"Yeah. My little sister threw my shoe into the garden, and I was trying to find it and there was this duckling in there."

"And it's been following you ever since?"

"Whenever it can, I guess. I stopped going into the backyard after it tried to bite my ankle."

Abby smiles with great satisfaction. "Ever heard of 'imprinting'?"

"No."

"Whoever a duckling sees first, it thinks is its mother. This duck isn't chasing you. It's following you because you're its mommy!"

And with that Hugo explodes into laughter.

"Shhhhh!" I say as Mr. Armstrong steps out of the classroom. He looks over in our direction as though he hears something. Hugo manages to muffle his hysteria. Abby smiles smugly. I glare at them both in disgust.

Mr. Armstrong walks across the courtyard with a pile of papers under his arm. The photocopy room is that way, so I guess he could be doing that (or destroying secret documents). It doesn't really matter, because all I care about is that he's not in the classroom. Time for us to investigate.

"Let's go!"

25

Time for a little Spider-Man action!

As we creep toward the classroom door, making sure no other teachers are around, I run through the plan again in my head. Hunt around Mr. Armstrong's desk until we find evidence that he is rigging the election. Take that evidence to Mrs. Sniggles, and then get Mr. Armstrong fired for interfering with the democratic process.

Simple enough, except ... he's locked the door.

Not so simple.

Hugo tries the windows next to the door, but they're locked too. This plan could be over before it's even started.

"Maybe we should just give up and regroup," Hugo says.

I'm already looking up at the high window on the side of the classroom. It's so high that Mr. Armstrong uses a pole to open it on hot days. It's also so high that sometimes he forgets about it and it stays open. Like it is today.

"We're not giving up," I say.

I run to the tree that stands alongside the building. I have no idea how this is going to work,

but there's only one way to find out. I begin to
climb. First the low branches, then shimmying
up the trunk a little, swinging from one branch
to another, getting higher and higher.

My shoelaces are undone, which doesn't
really help, but eventually I make it up so I'm
level with the window.

I thought I'd be able to reach. Turns out I'm going to need to jump because I have short arms to match my stumpy legs.

I love you, Mom! I love you, Dad! And Rosie! Here goes nothing ...

I jump and time slows down. I feel my feet leave the tree. My arms stretch out toward the window. There's a slight breeze. I look down. And down. And down. And realize I am going to die.

Bang!

I slam into the window ledge and somehow manage to hold on. I swing my leg up onto it. It's not graceful, but I made it! I actually made it! Jeepers.

Below me I see Hugo with his hands up in the air like he's saying a prayer. Abby is just shaking her head.

Inside, I lower myself down on top of a bookshelf. From there I can hop onto a display table and then onto the floor.

I run over to the classroom door and open it for Hugo and Abby.

WE DON'T HAVE LONG!

I close the door before my duck can get inside, then start to open the drawers of Mr. Armstrong's desk. Pens and pencils, staplers and a stress ball. Packets of protein-shake powder and power bars. The third drawer is locked.

Hugo opens up the cupboard and goes through the shelves. Abby is looking through Mr. Armstrong's trophy cabinet.

But there's nothing around that makes him look guilty of anything other than being super keen on going to the gym – a line of water bottles, a sneaker he saved from when he finished his first marathon. (So gross!) It sits on its own stand next to a framed postcard signed by Arnold Schwarzenegger.

There has to be something in that locked third drawer.

"Everyone look for a key," I whisper. I check under the desk, under the chair, behind some books, in the other two drawers, and in his little pink pencil case. Nothing.

Just as I'm about to give up, I look up at the marathon sneaker. Surely not? Can't be. He wouldn't. Would he? There could be all sorts of funguses in there. I'll never be able to wash the stink off ... Suck it up, Max. This is war.

I climb up on his chair to reach the sneaker. "Got it!"

I jump off the chair, put the key in the third drawer's lock, and open it.

"Oh." I had been hoping to find all my torn-up posters, but all that's inside is a large, bright pink box. It looks exactly like the ballot box sitting on the front of Mr. Armstrong's desk. "It's just another ballot box."

Abby comes over. "Open it up."

I lift the top off the box and we see that it's full of folded pieces of paper. I pick one up and unfold it.

"It's a ballot paper," whispers Abby. She's right. It's a slip of paper with all the candidates' names in a list. It's exactly the sort of form I would expect us all to use to vote on Monday.

Only this one has a big tick next to Layla's name.

I grab a handful and so do Hugo and Abby. As we flick through them, we see that Layla's name has been ticked on nearly every one.

"Fake ballot papers," says Abby. "He's going to switch the box after we vote."

"It doesn't matter what we do or how people vote," I realize. "Layla is going to win."

"Isn't this the evidence we were looking for?" Hugo asks.

"Not quite. We can't just take this to Mrs. Sniggles. We broke into the classroom to find it," I say, realizing too late that our plan has had a critical problem all along.

"And if we get rid of it, he'll know that we've done it before the vote and he'll just find another way," Abby says.

"Then we have to catch him in the act," Hugo says.

It's the first smart thing Hugo's said all day.

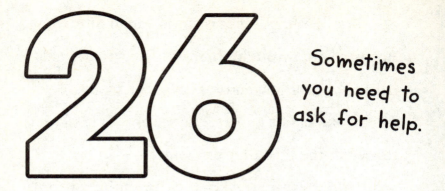

26

Sometimes you need to ask for help.

Monday. Election Day.

Hugo, Abby, and I have spent the weekend coming up with a plan. I'm not entirely convinced it's going to work, but I don't have any other options. I put on my favorite red-and-white-striped T-shirt. I even brush my hair. May as well look the part.

"Mom! Dad! Time to go!" I'm by the door.

Mom staggers out of her bedroom, her hair looking like a distressed skunk.

"Max, it's five a.m.!"

"Just want to be ready, Mom. Just want to be ready."

She looks at me in the way only your mom can look at you when you're about to do something that might just get you kicked out of school forever. Another moment and I would have confessed to everything.

Instead she asks: "Are you nervous, Max?"

I nod. "I guess a little."

Mom makes me a cup of warm milk and while she has a shower I open my back door and sit down on our step.

It doesn't take long.

Quack.

This time I don't run away. I stay nice and still. The duck waddles up to me, watching me intently. It walks right up onto my step, and then it sits down next to me.

"Today's a big day, Duck," I say. "I'm going to need your help. Do you think you can help me?"

It stares at me with its big dark duck eyes.

Quack.

I'm pretty sure that's a yes.

"Okay, let's practice. Now when I say, 'Quack', you say –"

Quack.

Excellent.

27

This is it ...

By the time the bell rings for school, all the kids are already standing outside the classroom, waiting. Hugo slips out of the room and joins me and Abby just as Mr. Armstrong comes marching around the corner. He's checking the little contraption that tells him how many steps he's taken and starts to yell: "All right, mongrels –"

He stops cold, suddenly realizing that Mrs. Sniggles is also standing with us. She's wearing her safari suit and hat again, although this time she has a giant toy toucan attached to the hat. Both the principal and the toucan are staring at our teacher.

GLAD YOU COULD JOIN US, MR. ARMSTRONG.

"Ah, er, yes, all right, inside, everyone!" he stammers as he opens the door.

Once we're all seated, Mr. Armstrong explains how the election will work.

"Layla will speak first, then Abby, and then Max at the end." He holds up a pink ballot box and a stack of blank ballot papers. They look identical to the ones we found on Friday night. "You will all vote on these slips of paper and put them in this pink box. I will count them, and then we'll have our first class president. Any questions?"

None. Over to Layla.

Her speech goes something like this:

1. OH, HOW I LOVE MR. ARMSTRONG!

2. I WON THIS TROPHY AND THIS TROPHY AND THIS TROPHY ...

3. I JUST LOVE-LOVE-LOVE MR. ARMSTRONG!

4. AND THIS TROPHY ...

5. MR. ARMSTRONG IS THE BEST TEACHER IN THE KNOWN UNIVERSE.

6. I SHOULD WIN THE ELECTION BECAUSE I AM A WINNER AND WINNERS WIN.

7. MR. ARMSTRONG TAUGHT ME THAT. HE'S A WINNER TOO.

8. VOTE FOR LAYLA!

I can't tell you if there were more details in there. I wasn't really listening. I am way too nervous about my own speech.

Abby's up next. She keeps hers short and punchy:

MRS. SNIGGLES, MR. ARMSTRONG, FELLOW STUDENTS. I STAND BEFORE YOU TODAY, ASKING YOU TO MAKE ME YOUR CLASS PRESIDENT. I HAVE MANY ACCOMPLISHMENTS, JUST LIKE LAYLA, ALTHOUGH MOST OF THEM ARE NOT ON THE SPORTS FIELD. MINE ARE IN THE CLASSROOM AND IN MY SCHOOLBOOKS. THAT DOESN'T MAKE ME VERY COOL, BUT IT DOES MAKE ME CLASS PRESIDENT MATERIAL. I WOULD LIKE TO SERVE THIS CLASS BY BEING YOUR REPRESENTATIVE, SO IF YOU'D BE SO KIND, VOTE FOR ME.

It's the sweetest I've ever heard Abby be. She can really turn it on when she has to.

That's not a skill I have.

I look down at my notes. Down at the first sentence of my new speech. When I wrote this yesterday, I'd begun with: "I'd like to start with a joke."

Am I really going to do this? There's no turning back now.

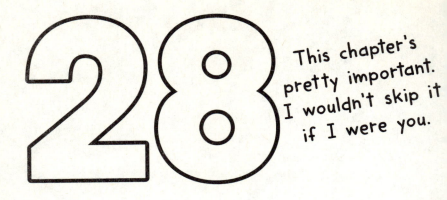

This chapter's pretty important. I wouldn't skip it if I were you.

"I'd like to start with a joke," I begin.

THERE ARE TWO DUCKS IN A POND. ONE DUCK SAYS, "QUACK!" THE OTHER DUCK SAYS, "THAT'S WHAT I WAS GONNA SAY."

There are a couple of laughs. Not many. This is a tough crowd.

I pause, awkwardly. Silence.

"I told you that joke because in election speeches, everyone always says the same thing. Things you've heard before. It gets so repetitive."

QUACK-QUACK-QUACK.

I say those last three words slowly and loudly. I wait again, hoping, but still there's nothing.

What if our plan doesn't work?

I look over at Hugo. He's sweating more than normal. It looks like he walked through a garden sprinkler on the way to school. I keep going, trying to buy some time.

"This election has been a little different though. For a start, two of our candidates aren't even here. Kevin got sick from Mr. Armstrong's smoothie, and Mr. Armstrong's catapult nearly took off Ryan's head. Accidentally, of course. And then there's a certain duck who always turns up at the wrong time."

Except for when you really need it to!

I glance over at Abby. I was never expecting to get this far along in my speech. I look down at my notes. If I keep going and publicly accuse Mr. Armstrong of cheating, in front of Mrs. Sniggles, without any evidence, then not only will I probably be kicked out of school, but I'll also look like a really sore loser. I'm not sure which is worse.

Abby smiles encouragingly, and I suddenly wonder if she knew the whole time that this plan wouldn't work.

I look back at Hugo. He's still sweating, but he's also nodding at me. One of his really expressive nods that tells me, "Go for it, Max. It's now or never."

You know what? Hugo's right. It's time to rise above the politics. It's time to tell the truth!

I look up from my notes. Let's do this.

> MR. ARMSTRONG TOLD ME THAT HE
> WOULD MAKE SURE I DID NOT WIN THIS
> ELECTION. THAT'S WHY HE TORE DOWN
> ALL MY POSTERS —

"Max!" The teacher stands up. I keep going.

> AND HE LIED ABOUT HAVING THE POOP
> VIDEO. HE HELPS LAYLA AND HE SABOTAGES
> EVERYONE ELSE.

"That's enough, Max!" declares Mr. Armstrong. "You're done!"

> MR. ARMSTRONG IS
> RIGGING THIS ELECTION!

ENOUGH!

The principal and her toucan leap to their feet. Everyone freezes. No one quite expected such an explosive voice from such a little person. The toucan glares at me.

"That is a very serious accusation, Max. Do you have any evidence?"

I look at Hugo and Abby. I'm done for. I can't tell Mrs. Sniggles about the ballot box without telling her we broke in. This plan doesn't work unless she finds it herself.

"Max?"

Who am I kidding? This plan was never going to work. I'm an idiot. I look out at the class and I can see they agree. This is worse than when Mr. Armstrong first said I did the poop.

It. Is. Over.

Quack.

I look up.

Did I just hear what I thought I just heard?

Quack.

Mrs. Sniggles looks confused. So does the rest of the class.

Quack.

It's the sound I've been desperately waiting for. Talk about cutting it close!

"What is that?" the principal asks. "It sounds like a duck."

Everyone looks around, trying to figure out where the noise is coming from.

IT SEEMS TO BE COMING FROM YOUR DESK, MR. ARMSTRONG.

Mrs. Sniggles steps forward, looking behind the desk, searching for the source of the quacks. Only Abby, Hugo, and I know exactly where the quacks are coming from. They're coming from where Hugo hid my duck before class.

Quack.

The principal presses her ear to Mr. Armstrong's third drawer.

Quack. Quack.

She tries to open the drawer. Locked.

"Mr. Armstrong, why is this drawer locked? Give me the key."

"Umm …" Now it's his turn to be speechless.

"The key, Mr. Armstrong."

He stammers, struggling for words. He looks like he could do with his stress ball right about now.

"There's nothing in there, Mrs. Sniggles," he manages finally. "It's Max! He was quacking all

through his speech. He's … umm … he's learned
to throw his voice! What do they call that kind of
comedian? A ventriloquist? Yeah, that's it!
Thinks he's a really funny
kid, this one."

THE KEY. NOW.

Mr. Armstrong glares at me, then
walks over to his trophy cabinet. He reaches
up into the stinky shoe and pulls out the key.
He glares at me some more before handing it over
to the principal.

Mrs. Sniggles unlocks the third drawer of the
desk. She carefully pulls it open. In a wild flurry
of feathers, Duck flies out, quacking happily.

As Duck does merry laps of the room, I watch as our principal reaches down and opens the second ballot box. She slowly picks up all the pre-ticked ballot papers. *Layla. Layla. Layla.*

Mr. Armstrong's eyes suddenly look very small. His face goes as white as an albino fur seal dressed like a ghost for Halloween.

The room falls silent and everyone holds their breath.

"Actually, Max, you can stay right where you are," Mrs. Sniggles says eventually.

MR. ARMSTRONG,
YOU COME WITH ME.

BALLOT

✓ Layla

✓ Kevin

BALLOT PAPER

✓ Layla

☐ Ke

☐ R

BALLOT PAPER

✓ Layla

☐ Kevin

☐ Ryan

Abby

Ma

BALLOT PAPER

✓ Layla

☐ Kevin

☐ Ryan

☐ Abby

☐ Max

BALLOT PAPER

✓ Layla

☐ Kevin

☐ R

Kevi

BALLOT PAPER

✓ Layla

☐ Kevin

R

Ab

Ma

vin

BALLOT PAPER

✓ Layla

☐ Kevin

☐ R

Ab

Ma

LOT PAP

Layla

☐ Kevin

☐ R

BALL

BALLOT PAPER

✓ Layla

☐ Kevin

☐ Ryan

Abby

Ma

BALLOT

LLOT PAPER

✓ Layla

☐ Kevin

an

LOT PAPER

✓ Layla

Kev

an

BALLOT PAPER

✓ Layla

☐ Kevin

Ryan

Layla
Kevin
Ryan
Abby
Ma...

BALLOT ...

BALLOT

Layla
Kevin
...an

BALLOT PAPER

Layla
Kevin
Ryan

Layla
Ke...
R...

BALLOT PAPER

Layla
Kevin
Ryan
Abby
Max

BALLOT PAPER

Layla
Kevin
Ryan
Abby
Max

BALLOT PAPER

Layla
Kevin
Ryan
Abby
Max

Kevin
yan
by
Max

a
Kevin
Ryan

29 She NEVER goes away!

A week later, Hugo and I are standing at the bus stop, waiting.

Our whole life feels like waiting.

Waiting for grown-ups, buses, holidays, dinner ...

"Our new teacher starts today," Hugo says. "I heard she's really nice."

Mmm, dinner. I wonder what's for dinner?

"Are you listening to me, Max?"

Maybe we'll have the chicken wings with the spicy stuff on them.

"Max?"

Mmmm ... chicken.

WELL, IF YOU'RE NOT LISTENING TO ME, NOW MIGHT BE A GOOD TIME TO GET SOMETHING OFF MY CHEST.

I could probably run to the work shed and ask Dad to make the chicken wings and still be back in time for the bus.

"I did the poop."

If I ran really fast ... Hang on.

"What?"

Hugo is looking sheepish – like a sheep who did a poop in the storeroom.

"It was me. I had to go into the storeroom to get something, and I'd had your dad's chicken wings the night before. You know the ones with the spicy rub?"

"Yes, I know the ones! I was just thinking about them!"

"Well, they always make me poop! It came on really quickly. I didn't have time to make it to the bathroom, and I didn't know what to do …"

"So you pooped on the floor?" I'm horrified.

"It's not as crazy as it sounds!" Hugo protests. "You should have been there!"

I DEFINITELY SHOULD NOT HAVE BEEN THERE! WHY DIDN'T YOU TELL ME?

Hugo looks down at the footpath. "I was embarrassed," he says. "You'd be embarrassed if you'd pooped in the storeroom."

"I was embarrassed because people THOUGHT I pooped in the storeroom!"

Hugo nodded. "Yeah. Thanks for covering for me. You're a good friend."

Grrrrrrr ...

MORNING, IDIOTS!

Abby Purcell. Just what I need.

"Morning, Madam President," Hugo says.

Oh, did I forget to tell you? Must have slipped my mind. Abby won the election. After they fired Mr. Armstrong, Mrs. Sniggles came and taught us for the rest of the week. She ran the vote. Ryan and Kevin got to run, as did Layla, because she'd actually had no idea about Mr. Armstrong's schemes. Not that it made any difference. Abby kicked our butts.

To be honest, I wasn't quite as disappointed as I thought I'd be. I'd wanted to be president to beat Mr. Armstrong, and I'd done that. Plus, who really wants to be in politics anyway? What a bore!

In Abby's acceptance speech, she said that Mr. Armstrong had been beaten by the funny kid and everyone gave me a cheer. I'll settle for that. Then she started yammering on about something to do with paper airplanes. Seriously, Abby, who cares?

"It's a lovely day to be alive, don't you think?" she is saying. "The day is filled with possibility!"

Actually, it will probably be filled with spelling tests and a history lesson, but I'll let her have her delusions.

"Oh, I forgot!" Abby says, and hands me a piece of paper. "I got this for you."

I look down at the flyer.

REDHILL TOWN TALENT QUEST!

Enter to raise money for charity and you might just become famous!

"I thought you might want to enter. You can tell your little jokes or something," Abby says.

Ooh, interesting. I would like to be famous.

Grrrrrrr.

Abby Purcell, you're going to ruin my life.

THE END

Did you enjoy
FUNNY KID FOR PRESIDENT?

Email Matt and let him know
what you thought!

matt.stanton@gmail.com

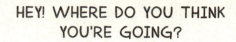

Look out for more adventures
with Max in
FUNNY KID: STAND UP!

Thank you!

Making a book is hard work, but the great thing is, you don't have to do it all by yourself. So this is a really good spot for me to say thank you.

The first person to thank is Beck, who just happens to be my best friend. She's so much of a best friend that she let me marry her. I get to see her every single day, which is just the best. If I didn't get to do anything fun ever again, not for the rest of my life, but I still got to see her every day, that would be fine with me. Some people say you shouldn't work with the person you're married to, but I think that's dumb. Working with Beck makes me better, and who wouldn't want to be better? We run a company together that creates stories for kids, so you'll hear lots more from us. The most awesome thing about working with your best friend? Going to work and coming home are both the best parts of the day.

I think kids are pretty great. In fact, they're the best sort of human, I reckon. The most awesome ones live in my house. They're called Bonnie and Boston, and they hired me to work for them as their dad. Hopefully I never ever get fired because this is the best job in the world. It's even better than getting to make funny books. I love them so much it makes my tummy do a little dance.

I have parents and a sister too. They are ridiculously encouraging. They make me think I can do anything, so I think I will. I wouldn't be doing this crazy job if they hadn't told me that I could. So thanks, guys!

Did you know that when you publish a book

you get to work with these people called editors? It's like having someone mark your homework and show you everything you need to fix *before* you have to give it to the teacher. You'd get 100% every time! Well, I've been able to work with two – Kate Burnitt and Jessica Dettmann. They're both absolutely brilliant and made this book so much better. And if I spelled their names wrong, it's their fault for not checking properly.

Not only do you get to work with editors, you get to work with a whole team of amazing people who know lots about making great books for kids. Like Michelle Weisz, Holly Frendo, and Bianca Fazzalaro, who know all these awesome ways of telling kids that there are new and exciting books to read. They're brilliant. Then there are people like Amy Fox who find really good bookshops to put the books in so that you can find them easily. She's tops at that. Elizabeth

O'Donnell is great at seeing if any other kids around the world would like to read the books. She found a whole bunch of other kids who are going to read Funny Kid so you should definitely give her a high five. Alice Karsen helps all of these people do their very busy jobs, which makes her the busiest out of all of them. I think she's okay with this, though, because *she* knows that *they* know that they couldn't possibly do it without her.

The top dog of the HarperCollins Australia Children's Books team is Cristina Cappelluto. She gets a huge thank-you because she lets us all do the thing that we love to do, which is make great books for kids. Also, if anything goes wrong, it's ultimately her problem, and that makes me breathe *so* much easier!

There are these amazing people who work on Funny Kid in other parts of the world.

Brilliant people like David Linker, Joe Merkel, Andrea Vandergrift, Rachel Denwood, and Harriet Wilson.

Working with all these people is fantastic, but there's one person in particular who you feel is your partner in crime. That person is called your publisher, and in my case, I got really lucky because my publisher is Chren Byng. Chren works with me on everything. She hatches plans, comes up with ideas, improves my jokes, hatches more plans, makes sure I don't sound stupid, chills me out when I start to sound crazy, and basically, besides Beck and me, she's Funny Kid's biggest champion. It's like having your coach, your star player, your cheerleader, and your playmaker all being the same person. "Thank you" are two words that don't feel like they quite cut it.

I made Funny Kid for funny kids, and I've met thousands of you (and your teachers) on the road. If this book made you smile, even just once, then I've done my job. The world is an amazing place – wonderful and sometimes scary, hilarious and sometimes sad. Making each other smile once in a while is a pretty special gift, so I hope I've shared that with you just as much as you share it with me.

I look forward to sharing more stories with you soon!

Matt Stanton, 2017

Matt Stanton is a bestselling children's author and illustrator, with over a quarter of a million books in print. He is the cocreator of the megahits *There Is a Monster Under My Bed Who Farts* and *This Is a Ball*. His much anticipated middle grade series, Funny Kid, launched around the world in 2017.

mattstanton.net

Books by Matt Stanton

Funny Kid for President

With Tim Miller:

There Is a Monster Under My Bed Who Farts

There Is a Monster Under My Christmas Tree Who Farts

There Is a Monster on My Holiday Who Farts

The Pirate Who Had to Pee

Dinosaur Dump

With Beck Stanton:

This Is a Ball

Did You Take the B from My _ook?

The Red Book

With Mark Carthew:

The Moose Is Loose!